ANN ARBOR DISTRICT LIBRARY

31621009732211

S0-ACU-901

Plop was a baby barn owl. He was
the same as every other baby barn owl—
except for one thing . . .

Plop was afraid of the dark.

Ann Arbor District Library

Text copyright © 1968 by Jill Tomlinson
Illustrations copyright © 2000 by Paul Howard
Text first published 1968 by Methuen & Co. Ltd.
Abridgment by permission of the Estate of Jill Tomlinson
First abridgment published 2000 by Mammoth, an imprint of
Egmont Children's Books Limited, 239 Kensington High Street,
London W8 6SA

All rights reserved.

First U. S. abridged edition 2001

Library of Congress Cataloging-in-Publication Data is available.

Library of Congress Catalog Card Number 00-052327

ISBN 0-7636-1562-5

2 4 6 8 10 9 7 5 3 1

Printed in Hong Kong

This book was typeset in Horley Old Style.
The illustrations were done in pastels.

Candlewick Press
2067 Massachusetts Avenue
Cambridge, Massachusetts 02140

visit us at www.candlewick.com

For Philip
and, of course, D. H.
J. T.

For Samuel
P. H.

CANDLEWICK PRESS
CAMBRIDGE, MASSACHUSETTS

The
Owl
Who Was
Afraid
Of the
Dark

Jill Tomlinson

illustrated by

Paul Howard

"The dark is *scary*," Plop told
his mommy. "I don't want to be
a night bird."

"I think you'd better find out
more *about* the dark first,"
Mommy Barn Owl said. "Ask
that boy down there."

Plop took a deep breath, and
down he flew.

"Hello!" said Plop. "I've come to ask about the dark."

"Oh, the dark is *exciting*," said the boy. "Especially tonight. We're having fireworks. Why don't you watch?"

"Does it have to be dark?" asked Plop.

"Of course!" the boy said. "You can't *see* fireworks unless it's dark!"

Back at the nest, Plop said, "I still do not like the dark *at all*, but I will watch the fireworks if you will sit by me."

"We will sit by you," said Mommy and Daddy Barn Owl.

And that is what they did.

Plop liked the fireworks
very much, but he was still
afraid of the dark.

The next afternoon, Plop flew down beside an old lady
in a lawn chair.

"Hello!" he said. "I've come to ask about the dark. I want
to hunt with my mommy and daddy, but they go in the dark,
and I'm afraid of it."

"How very odd," said the lady. "Now, I love the dark.
The dark is *kind*. I can forget that I am old, and I can sit and
remember the good times."

"Hmmm," said Plop. "I'll remember that."

And he flew back to tell his mommy about the kind
old lady.

That evening, while his parents were away hunting, Plop flapped down to join a Boy Scout.

"Hello!" Plop said. "Do you like the dark?"

"The dark is *fun!*" said the boy. "We're going to make cocoa and sing around the campfire when my friends get back with the wood. You should stay."

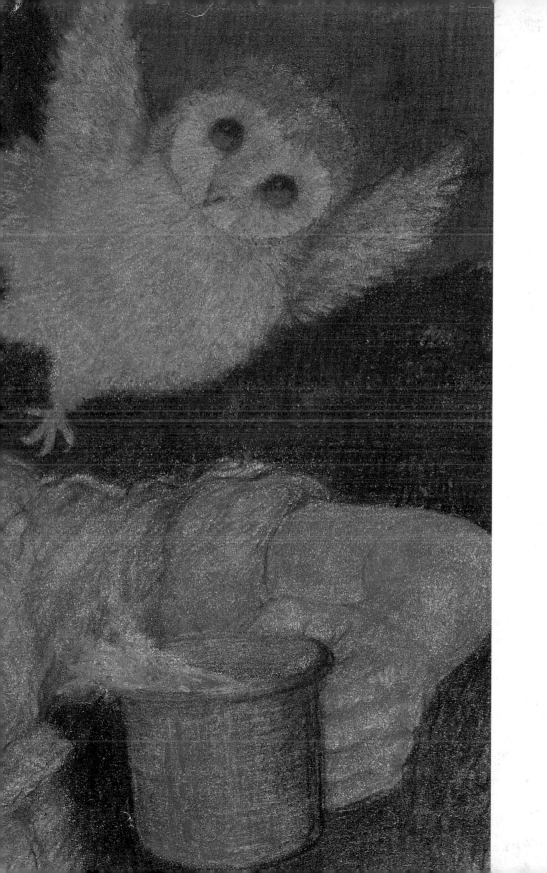

And so . . . Plop stayed.

The next day, Plop fluttered and flapped and landed with a plop beside a little girl. "Do *you* like the dark?" he asked.

"Of course I do!" said the girl. "The dark is *necessary*. Otherwise, Santa wouldn't come. You'd have an empty stocking on Christmas Day."

"I don't have a stocking," said Plop.

So the girl gave him her sock.

Plop thanked her and flew back to show his mommy.

In the evening, Plop woke
his daddy with a shout. He was
in a hurry to get up.
Daddy Barn Owl sighed.
"Wait until dark, Plop."
Plop did his best to
be patient.

When his parents went hunting that night, Plop flew down
and perched on a man's shoulder. "I don't like the dark,"
he said.

"Really?" asked the man. "But the dark is *wondrous*.
Look through the telescope."

Plop saw lots of stars and the patterns they made in the sky.
The man pointed out the Big Dipper, the Dog Star, and
Orion the Great Hunter.

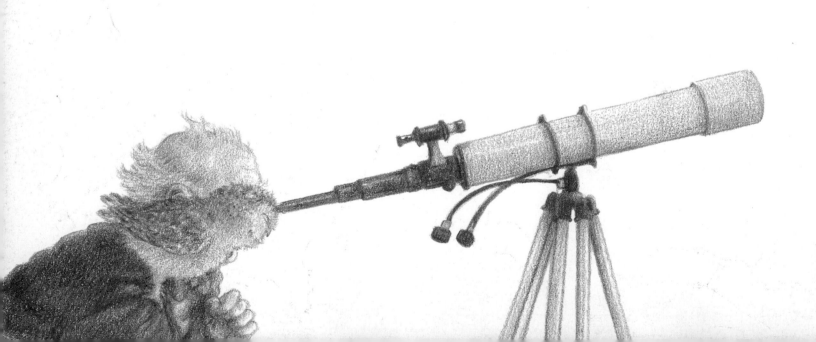

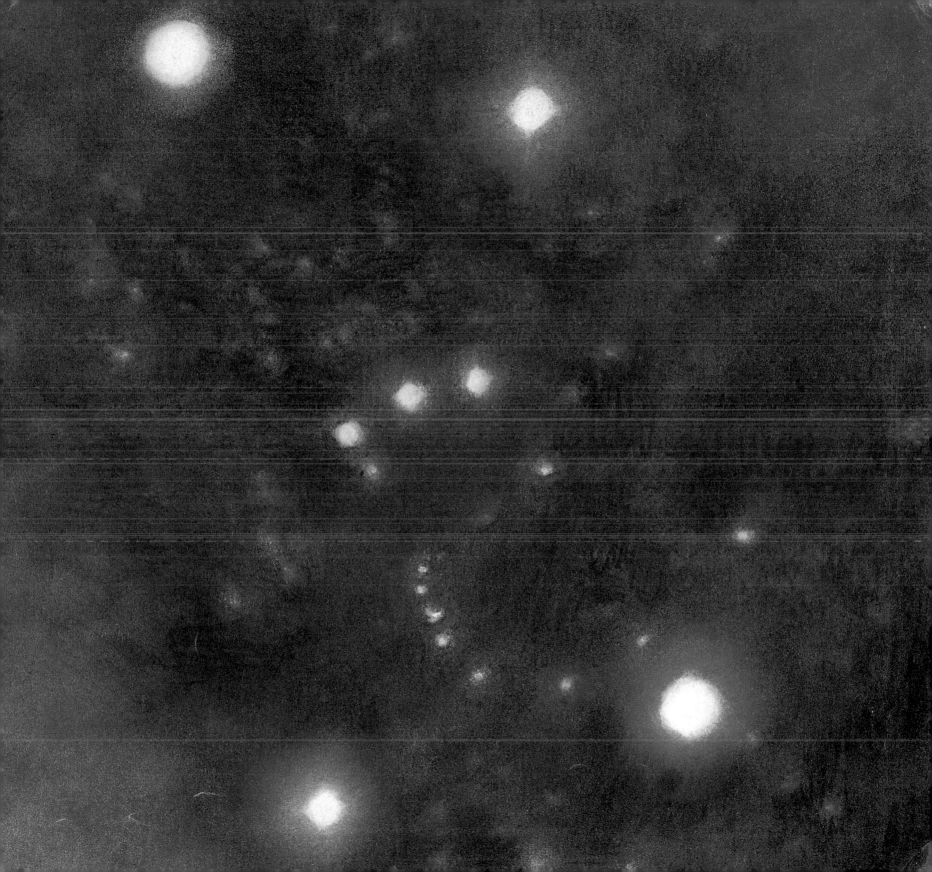

Later, Plop told his mommy and daddy about the telescope and the stars.

He dozed off at dawn and slept all day, just like a real night bird.

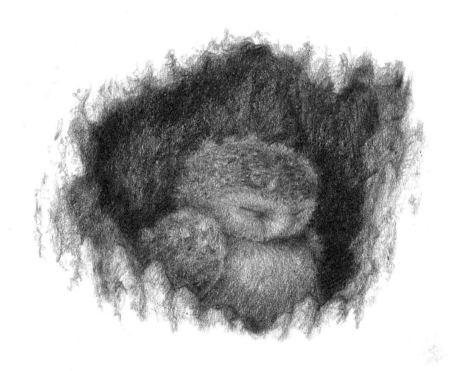

When he woke, it was almost dark again.

"Now who's a day bird!" Plop shouted at his sleepy parents.

He wasn't going to wait around for *them*. He might miss something!

Plop fluttered down and met a black cat under the tree.

"Hello!" said the cat. "I was just going exploring. Would you like to come along?"

"I'd like that very much," Plop replied. "But I'm afraid of the dark."

"The dark is *beautiful*," the cat said. "Come on. I'll show you."

The cat led Plop up to the rooftops, and they looked over the sleeping town. Plop thanked his friend.

"You're right. It *is* beautiful," he sighed. "This is *my* world. I'm a night bird!"

And Plop flew straight back to tell his mommy and daddy.

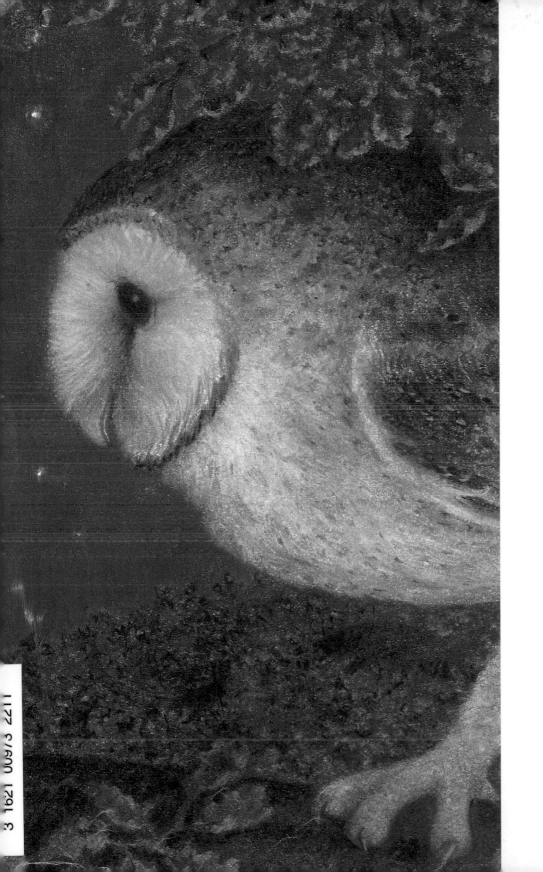

3 1621 00973 1277

Plop took a deep breath: "The boy said the dark is *exciting*. The old lady said the dark is *kind*. The scout said the dark is *fun*. The girl said the dark is *necessary*. The man said the dark is *wondrous*, and the cat said the dark is *beautiful*."

Plop looked up at his parents with twinkling eyes. "And *I* say the dark is *just right*."

Off they flew, Mommy Barn Owl, Daddy Barn Owl, . . .

and Plop in the middle . . .

Plop—the night bird.